| DATE | | | |
|------|------|------|------|
|  |  |  |  |
|  |  |  |  |
|  |  |  |  |
|  |  |  |  |
|  |  |  |  |
|  |  |  |  |
|  |  |  |  |
|  |  |  |  |
|  |  |  |  |
|  |  |  |  |
|  |  |  |  |
|  |  |  |  |
|  |  |  |  |

DEC - - 2022

Published by Tin House, Portland, Oregon
Distributed by W. W. Norton & Company

Library of Congress Cataloging-in-Publication Data
Names: Ferrada, María José, 1977– author. | Bryer, Elizabeth, 1986– translator.
Title: How to turn into a bird / María José Ferrada ; translated by Elizabeth Bryer.
Other titles: Hombre del cartel. English
Description: Portland, Oregon : Tin House, [2022]
Identifiers: LCCN 2022026733 | ISBN 9781953534460 (paperback) |
          ISBN 9781953534545 (ebook)
Subjects: LCGFT: Novels.
Classification: LCC PQ8098.416.E77 H6613 2022 | DDC 863/.7—dc23/eng/20220607
LC record available at https://lccn.loc.gov/2022026733

Printed in the USA
Interior design by Diane Chonette
www.tinhouse.com

# HOW TO

# TURN

# INTO

# A BIRD

## MARÍA JOSÉ FERRADA

TRANSLATED BY ELIZABETH BRYER

 TIN HOUSE / Portland, Oregon

*For Rodrigo Marín*

*Against all my better judgement,*
*I wanted to be happy.*

GÜNTER GRASS, *The Tin Drum*
Translated by Ralph Manheim

# FIRST WEEK

# MONDAY

**RAMÓN CLIMBED UP** the Coca-Cola billboard near the highway one Monday. That evening, as the sun was disappearing behind the hills that surround the housing complex, he decided he would stay. Even though it was late, the air was still warm. It was a heat that seemed even drier in this patch of the city, which had missed out on its share of pavement and trees because there had not been enough to spare.

"A desert," he said. And he realized that the hulking iron structure, which reminded him of a mammoth's skeleton, was big enough for furniture to fit inside: a mattress beneath what five million years before had been ribs, a table and a couple of chairs where the clavicle was, and a small lamp in the eye socket. He would rig up a water system by following the lattice of what had once been an immense forest of veins and nerves.

# TUESDAY

**WITH THE HELP** of several ropes and a pulley system he invented himself, he moved from his apartment to the billboard in record time: no more than three or four hours. When he finished, he uttered words that he alone heard, because, up there, in addition to having a panoramic vista of the city, Ramón was just the way he liked to be: alone.

Pictured on the billboard was a giant woman. The convertible she was driving was the same shade of red as the can of soda, and one of its doors had white lettering that read: OPEN HAPPINESS.

The light in the billboard house blinked on at around ten, right in the hole of the letter *O*. I remember because it coincided with the moment when I switched off my lamp.

"Get to sleep, Miguel."
"Yes, Mother," I said.

But instead of obeying, I pressed my ear against the wall and listened to Ramón's story.

**THE PERSON TALKING** on the phone in the apartment next to ours was my aunt Paulina, my mother's sister, who had lived with Ramón for ten years (I am twelve). Ramón, Paulina was saying, would be paid the same amount he had earned at the PVC factory, where he had worked from eight to six, Monday to Friday. As for the billboard, he could go up it whenever he felt like it.

Did they make him sleep up there? No, he slept up there because he wanted to. Was he employed by Coca-Cola? No, he was employed by a company that erected billboards beside highways all over Latin America. Were there any more job openings? In all honesty, she didn't know. Had Ramón finally gone mad all the way? That was a question best put to him, not her.

**THE TELEPHONE WOULDN'T** stop ringing, so I fell asleep to the sound of my aunt Paulina repeating the story, and I dreamed about a man who tossed bags of cash from a helicopter. The salaries—that was what was inside the bags—fell onto billboards: Nike, Panasonic, Ford, Gillette, Nestlé, L'Oréal, which were dotted across different capitals: Santiago, Lima, Buenos Aires, Managua, Mexico City. I was seated inside the helicopter and noticed that the billboards had something in common: it didn't matter which city they had been erected in, all of them were beside highways that led to an airport. Inside the dream, I knew I was dreaming, because even though wind was coming through the helicopter window, the hat worn by the man dispensing the cash didn't move.

# WEDNESDAY

**RAMÓN CALLED HIS** new boss to tell him that he had decided to fill his new position twenty-four hours a day, seven days a week. Was that a problem? The first three calls went straight to a recorded message that said the voice mail was not enabled. On the fourth attempt, his boss, one Eliseo, answered:

"Let's see if you've understood, Raúl."

"Ramón."

"Let's see if you've understood, Ramón: Your job is to take care of the billboard. To make sure the lamps aren't filched. If that means you need to sleep up there, swing from a cloud, or hide in the bushes, in all honesty we don't care."

"Okay, thank you," said Ramón, who considered what he had just heard a kind of municipal permit to reside in his new dwelling.

"Thank *you*, Raúl, thank you."

I was eleven years old, and I didn't need to be twelve to know the logical thing would have been to make that call before he moved to his new house, not after. That was eleven years of living in my building, in the housing complex, and in this world—long enough to realize that logic wasn't of much concern to many people around here. Least of all to Ramón.

A contract? They wouldn't sign a contract, but they would give him pay stubs. It was all the same to him, because in the PVC factory—as in all factories where the owner was the one ensuring compliance with labor regulations and paying the salaries—he'd had a contract that acknowledged only half the paycheck he collected. The rest? A "bit on the side."

Lunch wouldn't be provided, so he would have to cook it himself with the help of a gas cylinder and a camp stove. But this didn't represent a major change either: As far as he knew, lunch was only ever provided in the factories that had more than a hundred workers. Or in the movies. Although, come to think of it, factory workers never appeared in movies. Police or emergency services workers were preferred.

Half a contract and lunch. He had lost more in the war, Ramón thought as he swept away the remains of the mosquitoes, crispy and suicidal, that acted contrary to all theories about survival instincts in the animal kingdom to launch themselves at the lamps every night like tiny kamikazes.

# THURSDAY

**THE HOUSING COMPLEX** consists of a dozen buildings. Seen from afar—from the sky, for example—they look like enormous Lego bits. Each of them has four stories of four apartments. Depending on where the apartments are located, their respective windows overlook the stairwells, the walls, the sports court, or the highway. In moments of boredom, I've tried to count those windows. Owing to my failure to concentrate, I imagine, the result has always fallen somewhere between 300 and 330.

But the main thing is not the exact number of windows but the time of day when the neighbors—men, women, children—gaze through them. They do so out of nostalgia for the view they once had of the sun sinking between the hills, a view hidden by the billboards years ago. Or maybe, come to think of it, gazing at the horizon is just a signal announcing that another "goddamn day" is finally over. They have their reasons. The main thing is that looking out those windows was how the neighbors noticed there was a house inside the Coca-Cola billboard. From the outset, opinions were divided:

Some neighbors went "Ha, ha, ha" and deep down wanted to say—without actually taking the risk of doing so—that Ramón was a moron. Some neighbors asked, "What's he doing up there?" trying to provoke a knowing response that would confirm the smirking individuals' hypothesis: "Yes, he's a moron." A third, more serious group existed, and they went straight for a psychiatric diagnosis: "He's mad." "And what difference is there between a madman and a moron?" "Zilch." When they reached that point, they would have come to a unanimous agreement if it weren't for a few who chimed in at the last to say: "He can live wherever he feels like." Those holding the majority view pretended they hadn't heard. Finally, some neighbors expressed no opinion at all.

The history of humankind demonstrates that the people heading and closing that list—the ones who laugh, the ones who remain silent—turn out to be the most dangerous. But that history is not of too much concern to us here, so, for the moment, while faces are appearing at the building windows "just to take a look," the truth of the matter is that there is nothing to worry about.

# FRIDAY

"**HOW DO YOU** get up to the billboard?" I asked.

"Flying, Miguel, how else?" Paulina said as we climbed the same stairs where I sometimes sat to wait for her. She was joking, because really you could reach the billboard house via a ladder. In contrast to the stairway that connected the building floors, the ladder could be blocked with two planks in the form of a cross whenever Ramón didn't want to be bothered by the people down below.

"Are we the people down below?" I asked, curious.

"What do I know, ask him."

"Can we?"

"Can we what?"

"Go ask him."

"No, Miguel, it's dangerous."

"Why?"

"Because as far as I'm aware, you don't have wings, and if you fell you could split your head open."

"Does Ramón have wings?"

Paulina went quiet. Ramón didn't have wings, or if he did have a pair concealed beneath his shirt, then they were delicate wings that just about any wind could break.

"Can we go tomorrow?"

"You're such a pain, Miguel."

"Please, Pauli."

# SATURDAY AND SUNDAY

**BY THE TIME** Sunday came to an end, I'd convinced Paulina to take me up the billboard, and I don't think my persistence was the only reason she gave in. From the beginning, we knew Ramón wouldn't be there long. Some things you just know, and they are there to remind you that:

some things can't be explained
some things can't be divided
into what ends well and what ends
badly; some things can't be fixed

Like the billboard lamps that by the close of this story will end up broken. Or like everything up above that keeps turning: celestial bodies, cosmic matter. Sooner or later, they will cease to exist. Is that sad? "Sad, in practice, is your beer running out," Ramón would have said. And anybody listening would have looked at him as they always did: with a mixture of contempt and admiration.

# THE DAYS FOLLOWING

**HE WAS ODD,** but not a bad person. The problem, the real problem, said my mother, was that Ramón was "fond of a drop." You could see it in his glassy eyes and trembly hands, in the smell that by that stage emanated not from his mouth but from his pores. "Do you honestly not notice it, Pauli?" She asked the question not to hear the answer but because she wanted to annoy Paulina, who always ended up telling her, far too nicely for my liking: "Mind your own business."

"I only say it because I love you," my mother would respond. "I only say it because you mean so much to me." "I only say it because you're my little sister," she would go on. And finally, she would start weeping and saying that Paulina, Ramón, all the residents of the damn housing complex, my father (who had disappeared years before), and I were "such leeches, so ungrateful, so stupid."

Family. Around that time, I decided that this would be the title of the movie I would make one day. It would end with all the characters passing out beneath a table after drinking a thick, sugary liquid. My camera would focus on the label of the bottle, which would read: LOVE. The end.

Odd, but not a bad person. Ramón had heard that phrase ever since he was a boy.

Even back then he knew that if he wanted to listen to the birds perched atop the utility poles, he needed silence. Or, even more simply: when it came to talking and listening, he preferred to listen.

## HOW TO TURN INTO A BIRD

It wasn't a war against the universe. Or even a war against himself. Still, several people sustained injuries. The first was his mother. Odd: in all groups there is a misfit and right from the first she was sure her son would fill the quota. So, it was she and not he who suffered whenever his report card arrived from school: He has a good grasp of the curriculum. He takes care of his appearance. He neglects to participate in group activities. She, not he, was the one who gazed out the window at the children playing at a birthday party to which Ramón, once more, had not been invited.

At first, she made him go down. Told him to go play. See if next time they would invite him ("You have to make an effort, Ramón"). And without a word of protest, he would go down. But once he was there, instead of joining in he would stand still and look up: even though they shared a passing resemblance, the clouds scudding across the sky at that time of day were different from the ones he had seen the day before. Something similar happened with the colors: as the days went by, the landscape—if the scrubby hills surrounding the housing complex could be called that—underwent a slight change.

Soon before his ninth birthday, after once more seeing the disappointment on his mother's face as she read his report card, he decided to start making more of an effort. He went by his classmates' desks handing out small invitations to his birthday party. He would be waiting for them, his hair combed and the apartment full of balloons.

A couple of days later, while his mother was blowing up those balloons, she felt that her lungs were not the only things emptying a little. Her heart was too. What would happen if they didn't show?

## HOW TO TURN INTO A BIRD

Would it mean that Ramón, at all of nine years of age, had failed as a child? Was it his fault? Or, even worse, hers? But there was no need to search for answers because the guests arrived. And they played, laughed, and even broke apart a piñata.

While she listened to them, Ramón's mother was taken back to the day when she arrived from the south, Ramón a babe in arms, at one of the buildings of this very housing complex. Because even though the apartments were small, there were peculiar cases where hearts were big and families that were already squeezed for space welcomed newcomers, who settled in as best they could. Almost always, the expected stay of a few months stretched into years. And now here she was, watching time go by, together with this boy who was finally playing with everyone else. Her boy.

Little Ramón, who was starting to develop the habit of keeping his mind in several places at once, looked up at his mother peering out the window. Not letting his focus drift from the ball, he noticed her face was wearing something resembling a smile. He continued running and decided that if it meant he could keep seeing that smile on her almost-always-sad face, then he would keep making an effort, and would put a stop to his search for silence. Or, rather, he would put that search on hold.

Alcohol? He discovered it when he was a teenager. No big deal. Or it was: alcohol was a welcome discovery, a barrier he could erect between himself and the noise. And, like every alcoholic in the world, he was certain he could give it up whenever he wanted.

**I'M NOT SURE** how many times I visited the billboard. It must have been nine or ten. Sometimes with Paulina—one of the few people in whose company Ramón forgot his nostalgia for his mute childhood—other times alone, and a final time when the neighbors made me go, when Ramón was no longer there. I would have liked for there to have been more times, even maybe to have stayed and lived up there, but things don't always turn out the way you hope. If anything, they turn out completely different. The main thing is, we had enough time to talk a little. And to be silent and notice how, at the hour when the cars slow down, the wind starts blowing harder.

Relationships between what happens above and what happens below. Ramón was sure they existed. It had taken him thirty-six years to find the observatory he needed if he wanted to resume the search for silence he had interrupted when he was nine. An observatory, and a job that, without wasting his time, meant he could buy a good coat, and guaranteed him a bowl of rice. Beer, too.

There were threads, he explained. Delicate threads connecting things. That morning you happened to choose your blue shoes and at the exact moment when you were tying your laces, an astronomer discovered a couple of stars that, owing to their elevated surface temperature, shone with a bluish color. Had your choice helped, to some extent? In other words, could that discovery (a reminder: bluish stars) be the cosmic, spectral equivalent of your shoes? And, if that was the case, had you been right not to choose the black ones?

Relationships between what happens above and what happens below. You had to position yourself in an intermediary space—not too attached to the earth, not too close to the sky—in order to see them.

**AFTER CROSSING THE** highway that bordered the housing complex and walking along the edge of the canal, we arrived at the foot of the billboard for the first time. Paulina gave me two instructions: "You first," and "While you're climbing up, don't look down." Eager as I was to reach the top, I paid heed.

Ramón's new house was just as I had imagined it: a ramshackle nest. It looked like it had been made by a bird that wasn't all that interested in building a lasting monument to its species. The walls—except the one that was the billboard itself, which was the sturdiest of all, or the only sturdy one, really—had gaps between one plank and the next, and through those gaps, as I would notice as dusk fell, filtered the light. Holes, and through them came rays that illuminated just one object at a time: the mug sun, the coffee-jar satellite, the sugar-bag moon.

I remember Ramón greeted me as if my climbing up there were the most ordinary thing in the world, and after telling me to take a seat wherever I wanted (the chair or the floor), he asked Paulina about her day. She worked as a shelf stacker in the health and beauty section of Superior, the supermarket, so out of her mouth came words like "suntan lotion," "shelves," and "warehouse." Ramón, in turn, tried to explain the electrical system he had implemented, thanks to which we could enjoy an instant soup in another five minutes.

He didn't need to mention the small hoist—a wooden box tied to a rope that he could raise with the help of a handle—the express purpose of which was to bring up his beer. By prior agreement, one of his factory workmates went by the liquor store a couple of times a week and delivered Ramón his beer in exchange for a minimal commission that, rather than cash, consisted of three or four cans. To Ramón's surprise, the hoist could bear a good deal of weight, and it was as practical as a clock. When I first laid eyes on it, I thought something like it should be installed on the windowsills of all the world's buildings to make the lives of elderly citizens easier.

"A world unto himself," said Paulina, celebrating not the hoist but the soup, which had turned out well.

"What does that mean?" I asked.

"That you know how to make the soup you eat. And how to wash the bowl."

"So as not to bother anybody?"

"So nobody bothers you."

After eating the soup, and after I volunteered to wash the bowls amid the muddle of buckets, bottles, and hoses, we sat down to gaze at the landscape. Through the building windows we glimpsed the shadows of children, who at this time of night were protesting because bedtime was drawing near, as well as the shadows of adults, who, tired, collapsed in front of the television. There were shadows of grandparents too, which remained so still that they blended with the damp stains on the walls. A little higher up, the stars appeared, and were reflected in the water of the canal down below.

"What are you staring at?" Paulina asked Ramón.

"Two blue specks that weren't there yesterday," he said, sipping a little beer.

"Clouds must have been covering them."

"That must be it," responded Ramón, who among his arsenal of survival strategies had one that really served him: letting his conversation partner have the last word.

"That must be it," repeated Paulina, as if to remind him that after so many years spent by his side, she knew him as well as a person can know another—which is to say, more or less.

Before we climbed down, Paulina and I took a final look at the stars, an act that I replicated each time I went up there. On the way back to the housing complex, we played dog and blind man. It was simple: the dog, intelligent as it was, gave instructions—keep going, danger, turn right, watch out, stop, turn left. The blind man, who was almost always me, kept his eyes closed and followed.

The threads that connected things seemed to do so according to laws, and these laws worked like the ropes and pulleys Ramón had used to hoist his furniture. A little too much weight, or a fault in the weave of one of the ropes, could make the mechanism buckle, causing a table, a chair, or the whole sky to fall to the ground.

"Action and reaction," Ramón said to me one day.

"What does that mean?"

"That the earth is round and if you throw a stone hard enough, that same stone will hit you in the back."

"Nobody is that strong," I pointed out.

"Action and reaction," he said once more, not taking my counterargument into account.

And the thing is, Ramón made his infrequent conversations advance and recede, leaving ideas

unfinished only to return to them later, as if playing with a spring. A habit that, at that elevation,
and given the prospect of drinking without anyone
counting the empties, became more pronounced.
Instead of attributing it to indifference on his part,
I liked to think he had the ability to talk to others and to himself at the same time. I thought the
contradictions and the silences, which he wasn't
the least bit concerned to fill, were due to the
effort that this two-way communication involved.
Of course, there were also people who, not gloss-
ing it over, simplified the issue:

"He's mad," my mother said.

"Mad," agreed a neighbor, as she washed the
dishes in an apartment three floors above.

Thanks to a combination of human nature and
architectural flaws, the building where we lived,

like most buildings in the world, was a sophisticated system of echoes and resonances.

What someone said in the living room of 2B could be heard in the kitchen of 3D or 4A, owing to the thin walls and the shortcuts the construction company had taken on the plumbing and finishings. Words, snores, and complaints passed through the walls and traveled along internal highways at high speed. Factor in the interest human beings take in finding out what goes on in other people's homes, and the result was a free-of-charge, stifling communications network that in some ways resembled a spiderweb.

"Is he still there?" said somebody in 4B.

"Sure is," responded somebody in 3B.

The removal of one of the game pieces—Ramón— to a higher location did not mean that all the pieces below—my mother's increasing hostilities, school, Paulina's job—had stopped taking their course. What I mean is, while Ramón was beginning his new life in the billboard, we, along with everything else—and we were the people who made everything else move in one direction or another—kept going at our own pace.

**MY MOTHER OWNED** one of the small stores in the housing complex and was an active participant in the neighborhood council. In both places she felt that others took advantage, even though she was the one doubling prices in the first instance, and the one proposing the agenda in the second. There was a third place: the family, made up of Paulina, Ramón, the ghost of my father (who was still alive somewhere), and me. We only wanted to hurt her, she would say. With our presence, with our breath, with the dumb faces we wore whenever she had one of her fits of rage.

She had been responsible for Paulina after their mother died, and this was how Paulina repaid her.

Neither Paulina nor I understood what my mother piled inside that "this," but we both agreed that sometimes it's best not to ask.

And I was a load on her shoulders ever since the day my father stepped out, saying he would be right back. Like most of his kind (fathers), he never returned. So, my mother took sole responsibility for clothing and feeding me, and for something a little more nebulous that we could call my education. And for showering me with a love that could very quickly transform into hate.

I would have liked to ease her burden: Instead of two bread rolls I was happy to eat just one. And to pull on the same socks several days in a row to spare her unnecessary suffering, a suffering that, since my father's moron blood coursed through my veins, I felt partly responsible for. But did any of it help?

## HOW TO TURN INTO A BIRD

The overabundance of drama nurtured a creative vein, and this led us to put on shows that the neighbors watched, spellbound.

A voice-over says: "Your father's going to pay for this" (everything else, except for the noise of the plates and the music, will unfold like it does in silent movies).

1. My mother takes a plate and hurls it against the wall.

2. I slip out and ring the doorbell of the apartment next door.

3. Paulina, who lives there, opens the door and gestures in a way that means: Your mother is crazy.

4. Paulina closes the door and puts on loud music, to cover the sound of plates breaking.

5. I make out as if I forget the plates. Paulina acts as if nothing is happening, and eventually I forget in earnest, until my mother appears in the doorway and says: "Miguel, time for dinner."

The neighbors applaud, draw their curtains, and turn back to their television sets to watch a show about a man who communicates telepathically with animals.

I am the only one who sticks around for the final part of the show. My mother lies down, tired after dealing with customers all day (incapable of buying a whole kilo of anything, they make her

HOW TO TURN INTO A BIRD

portion everything into 250-gram bags); tired of dealing with me; and, most of all, tired of dealing with the distance between the image she has of herself and the one the rest of us have of her.

"Mirror, mirror," she says, with one foot in sleep, "who is the hardest working, the kindest, the strongest of them all?" And, instead of saying her name, the evil mirror responds: Paulina. Or, even worse, it names the woman who everybody says lives with my father only a few blocks from here. So, when the loving moans of the couple in 2A begin, she hears my father and "that slut." In her sleep she goes on fighting, and she hangs out a window in her dream to shout at them to be quiet. All afire as usual, they pay her no heed, so my mother decides to cut her losses: She opens the bag of rage she keeps inside and fills it a bit more. And a bit more.

**SCHOOL WASN'T THE** least bit important to me. Mind you, I went every day, sat in my seat, opened my textbooks, and wrote in my exercise books. My grades were average. I didn't make friends I would remember forever, but I knew enough people not to have to look on from the sidelines when they played ball at recess. I played, and if I needed to shove or elbow to make a corner kick, I shoved or elbowed. I kicked, too. I didn't have a favorite subject, but I did have a favorite time of day, which was when it was announced that school was out.

I wasn't a model student, but I was a good model of a typical student.

**WHENEVER PAULINA ARRIVED** at Superior, the first thing she did was arrange the Linden shampoos on the shelves. Fuchsia, orange, yellow, white, green. The visual display of that rainbow of plastic bottles was accompanied by the sound of the cash registers and the smell of the disinfectant used to clean the aisles, and together they worked a hallucinogenic effect on her:

That day, Ramón was in the billboard, raising a wire. In some part of the sky, the wire was hooked up securely enough that he could shinny up it. Ramón went up, up, up until he was lost in the darkness. Down below, a few dogs barked, and flashlights appeared, illuminating a fine rain of insect wings that disintegrated before they touched the ground.

As well as being spectacularly vivid, the trips were brief. Without leaving the supermarket, Paulina could find herself anywhere at all—from the main squares of foreign cities to scenes in films she had never seen. She would have liked to know if those trips were as real as they felt. To see if she really did appear as an extra in some of the films. It seemed like a good job, a dream, and Paulina walked into it as she did everything in life: not asking herself many questions, and not encountering too much resistance.

Unlike my mother, who insisted on being the center of everything, Paulina was a current that flowed over and around the hard facts and objects she bumped into in the supermarket aisle and on her life path, which for her were one and the same. This special talent of hers probably resulted from the physical work she did carrying boxes from the warehouse to the shelves. Or, more simply, it was a natural predisposition toward focusing on the problems of today, not on the problems of yesterday or the day after tomorrow.

No, it definitely didn't seem like a bad job, being an extra in a film, she thought as she straightened some bottles of suntan lotion. You walked along the same street the lead actor strolled down, or you sat at one of the desks in the main character's office, and at the end of the day you were paid for simply having been there.

Through my window, I saw Paulina climb up.

I couldn't hear anything, but I could imagine the conversations she had with Ramón:

"Why do you like it up here?" she would ask.

"Just listen," he would respond.

"All I can hear is a car moving away."

"There you have it."

**IN MOST PEOPLE'S** eyes, Ramón's temperament cried out to be interpreted. And as happens with all interpretations, those doing the interpreting invented whatever they felt like. At the PVC factory, where he had worked until a couple of weeks before, they said he was traumatized years earlier when the pipe cutter had confused the arm of a workmate with the pipe it was supposed to be cutting. The next day everybody was talking about the puddle of blood and how the man in question had lain writhing in it. It was a discussion they would repeat months later in the labor lawsuit, after the company had refused to pay for the prosthesis because the now one-armed man had been the fool, not the machine. Unlike everybody else, all Ramón remembered was the hoarse squeak the machine had let out as it split the bone.

"It was halfway between a tree creaking and a car screeching to a stop."

"Do you often listen to the creaking of trees?" the lawyer representing the company asked, hoping finally to find a mitigating factor in his client's favor.

"Sometimes," responded Ramón, oblivious to the lawyer's intentions. And then he added: "In autumn."

That noise of blade, bone, and cartilage had awoken Ramón's need for distance once more. If he had tried to explain why he found this noise so arresting, he would have said it was an echo of the noise he heard, at roughly five months' gestation, through the amniotic fluid in which he had been floating so pleasantly until then.

"The noise of the world," he explained to the psychologist who visited the factory after the incident. She spent twenty minutes interviewing each person who had been within an eight-and-a-half-meter diameter of the mishap, thanks to a pilot plan rolled out by the Workers Safety Agency.

"Would you like a referral to a psychiatrist?"

"There's no need for that," said Ramón.

"Any other complaints?"

"A bit of a headache most mornings."

"One last question: Do you feel the characters who appear on television are trying to talk to you?"

"No."

Water and aspirin, the psychologist recommended. And if the noise became a real bother, alprazolam. She would jot down the name of a place where he could buy it without a prescription.

Ramón heeded only the part about the water, not out of a desire to follow the psychologist's recommendation but more because it was a necessity signaled by his own body. He didn't need the aspirin and alprazolam, even less so now that his elevation put a natural barrier between him and everybody else.

"The noise of the world," Ramón would say to himself. Words of love. Particulars. Instructions. Recriminations. Laughs. Explanations. And a gunshot or two, which, amid all the auditory stimuli, you couldn't be sure was real.

"It's like they're stretching."

"Like what are?" asked Paulina.

"Sounds."

"Look at the stars. Look at the one peeking over that hill. Know what it's called?" asked Ramón.

"How would I know?"

"It's called Pauli."

"Yeah, sure."

"I'm the caretaker of all this. That means I get to decide the names, too."

"You're such a fool, Ramón."

They said something like that. And then they laughed and held hands.

**THE WHOLE TIME** Ramón was up the billboard, I was there too. Between one visit and the next, there was a space inside me that I filled with imaginary conversations and views of the city. Up to a few weeks previous, Ramón had been my aunt's husband, nothing more. But by climbing up to the billboard house, he had transformed into an intermediary figure somewhere between a friend, a bird, and a teacher. I'd never seen that combination before, and I would never see it again.

I was overcome by the mildly feverish state experienced by anyone who, from one day to the next, feels that their ordinary life has transformed into an interesting one (in those days, I felt I was

Ramón's accomplice as well as his friend). And in this state, instead of searching the dictionary for the meanings of words I was assigned for homework, I looked up my own.

Bird: A creature with feathers and wings, usually able to fly.
Man: A rational living being, male or female. Prehistoric man.

When my teacher demanded to know why I had arrived to class without my homework yet again, I didn't bother to answer. My classmates confused my silence—what could I say?—with some sort of rebellion. And then the thing that always happens around rebels happened: 30 percent were dubious, and 70 percent started to feel something like admiration. If there were forty-five students, you do the math.

**SOME NIGHTS THE** friend who delivered his beers or another of his factory workmates came by the billboard:

"You've got yourself a good setup here, Ramoncito."

After telling Ramón about their day, they always came to the question they wanted to ask: What did the job involve? Keeping an eye on the billboard lamps? It couldn't be that and nothing else. That would be too easy, too good to be true. And they had seen enough—disreputable factories, supermarkets, lobbies, kitchens—to know this was not how the world worked.

Their cigarettes, seen from afar, glowed like fireflies.

"And what do you do when the lamps aren't on?"
asked that night's skeptic.

    "I look at the sky."

    "Nice job, Ramoncito, nice job."

    "Cheers."

    "Cheers."

**THE CONVERSATIONS UP** the billboard overlapped the ones Paulina started having with herself. More than discussions, these were examinations of the past, to see if she could pinpoint the word or action that signaled the beginning of the distance she could now measure with a ladder.

It couldn't be said that she had neglected to notice.

For several nights now, she kept recalling a pair of snails that had been hidden in the vegetables she brought home from the market one day. She carefully placed them in a flowerpot in the kitchen. For hours on end, one followed the other and vice versa until, when they finally collided, they mated with a tenderness that comes naturally to small animals.

No, it couldn't be said that she had neglected to notice, she told herself with the calmness of those who don't ask for explanations, but don't offer any either.

Even a love such as that—small animals and human beings collided at this point in her thoughts—was bound by the laws of time. And time did what it knew best: it rolled on, not waiting for anybody.

This insistent recollection ended the moment the snails abandoned the hollow of earth and went on their way, in different directions, each of them toward the memory of the other.

**PRACTICAL AS SHE** was, after the abandoned-flowerpot vision, Paulina rolled all her questions into just the one: "Do you intend to stay up the billboard forever, Ramón?"

As could be expected, he said nothing. He knew that once trapped in words, the events that circulated in the air became a concrete presence. Or an absence, in his case.

I observed their silhouettes from my window, not to intrude upon their conversations or make up my mind as to whether Ramón was just another coward, but because I was checking that the billboard house was still there. And because I wanted to put my own threads in place, too. I was working on that, looking outside, when I saw a fire in the distance. Two adults and three children were standing around it, trying to ward off the cold. Scratch that, there wasn't just one fire, there were two, three, four, five, six, seven, and they were burning at what from this distance looked like the foot of the billboard.

"What are those lights over there?" asked my mother, who was spying through the other window.

"Fires," responded the neighbor from 4A.

"Just what we need," said somebody from 3C.

"I knew the billboard house was a sign that things were out of kilter, a bad omen," concluded my mother, who counted among her many occupations that of opening and closing conversations.

Both matters—the billboard house and the fires— would be raised for discussion at the neighborhood council meeting.

**ON MONDAYS, WEDNESDAYS,** and Fridays, Paulina finished her shift at Superior at six in the evening. On those days of the week, I went to meet her. I liked to go inside, because I could make the most of the situation to fill my kangaroo pocket with Sahne-Nuss bars, and because whenever her workmates saw me, they said: "Your son's getting so big!"

At first Paulina clarified that I was her nephew, but when the next time they saw me they reiterated that I was her son—and that I was getting big—she decided to let it slide.

"Are your workmates stupid?" I asked her one day.

"It must be the floor disinfectant; can't you smell it?"

"You can smell it from the housing complex, but what's that got to do with it?"

"Maybe it affects their memory. What was your name again?"

Paulina told me that when they complained about the smell to the aisle manager, he responded with one of the stories he liked so much—stories from real life. The disinfectant Lynox, which they bought in bulk, was made in Thailand. Each time the factory on the other side of the world produced enough of it to fill a new container—roughly 15,200 liters—a worker dropped dead, the cause of death something that exists only in Asian countries: death from overwork.

When certain products switched places—when sausages turned up on the wine shelf and cans of evaporated milk were found on the hand-cream display—these were not proof of frustrated attempts to steal but games played by the ghosts that had traveled inside the drums.

This method of motivating employees, which combined geographic components (the mention of far-off countries and a neighboring country or two) with features of the local imaginary (the appetite for devils, ghosts, and apparitions), had, in the words of a philosophy student who worked in the dairy section, a Socratic basis and sought to stimulate collective reasoning: Was this the worst spot on the map? Had anyone ever dropped dead at Superior from the smell of disinfectant? The answer in both cases was "no." Therefore, "Fewer complaints and more work," the aisle manager would say. "And whoever doesn't like it can find the door at the end of the grocery aisle, between checkouts four and six."

Paulina and her workmates could have cried, but most of the time they laughed. They didn't want to shatter the family fantasy they liked so much—they wanted the best for it, and that made it a family, even if all evidence suggested otherwise. So, whenever I made an appearance in the aisle, I would say to Paulina, "Hi, Mother," and wink. She would respond: "Hi, Son."

My brain, like most human brains, struggled to comprehend the very jokes it emitted, so once our game of pretend had begun, I developed something resembling the instinct of a child who fears abandonment. This meant I learned to read the looks Paulina exchanged with strangers.

"Hi, kid," the security guard said and pretended to search my backpack for the chocolate bars that were clearly stuffed in my pocket.

Paulina laughed. The guard laughed.

And I said nothing, but I looked at him with all the seriousness that my eleven years of age allowed me to muster.

"What's up with you?" asked Paulina when, as we walked from Superior to the billboard, she noticed I was sticking to my plan of not saying a word.

"What do you mean?"

"Can I have a Sahne-Nuss?"

"I don't have any." I grinned, and gave her a bar.

"Thief," said Paulina, and pulled a can of Sprite out of her backpack, one I hadn't seen her buy at the supermarket or in any of the kiosks around here.

**RAMÓN WAS JUST** the way we had left him days before: seated, gazing at the hills. We greeted him, and he looked at us as if he couldn't quite bring us into focus. The house was the same, except for a small, indoor hill formed by empty beer cans, a perfect complement to the landscape.

I don't know if he was happy to see us, or if he simply remembered that, like us, he was a human being, and every now and then, human beings need food. Whatever the case, he invited us to take a seat and added a cup of rice per head to instant soup. As a token of my thanks, when we finished the soup I placed the last of my chocolate bars on the table, and we had them with mugs of tea. Paulina was talking about their school days—as

well as neighbors, she and Ramón had been classmates after he, who was three years older, repeated
twice—when we heard children's voices in the
distance.

"They're playing, building a mud city," said Ramón.

"How do you know?" I asked.

"I hear a girl's voice saying, 'There's one house
too many'; 'We're short a street.'"

"Are they from the housing complex?" asked
Paulina.

"From the shanties going up beside the canal,
I think."

"Again?"

"Again."

There weren't six or seven fires, as I had counted
the day before from the vantage of my window,
but more than ten. When night fell, they twinkled,

as if they were all that remained of a tired star that had plummeted to Earth.

"The Homeless People's Star," said Ramón.

"When did they get here?" asked Paulina, as if they were talking about people they knew.

"A couple of days ago."

The children were now playing right below the billboard, and their voices reached us, carried on the wind:

"That roof's all wonky, and this house here needs a window," said the girl. She seemed to have all the know-how, and therefore to be in charge of doling out instructions to the two smaller boys who were playing with her.

"He always does it wrong," said one of the boys, motioning to the other with his head, not lifting his hands from the mud.

"You're the one doing it wrong," said the accused in self-defense.

The girl, who wasn't there to be a judge, only a construction manager, paid them no mind, keeping her focus on the city.

"Built like this, will it withstand the rain?"

The boys looked at her, not saying anything.

"Will it withstand a storm? An earthquake?"

One of them started wobbling as if the ground beneath his feet were moving. The other one followed suit, and then, after the imaginary disaster, the three of them cried out and burst into laughter.

## HOW TO TURN INTO A BIRD

When an hour later Paulina and I climbed down the billboard (carefully, not looking down), the children were still there. "Good evening," Paulina said, and the girl, whose face seemed familiar, looked at her but didn't say a word.

We skirted the canal and crossed the highway. Once in the housing complex, Paulina put a finger to her lips, making the gesture for "silence" to remind me of something so obvious that maybe it wasn't: better not tell anybody about our visits to the billboard house.

When I opened my apartment door, I had to face my mother:

"Where were you, Miguel?"
    "At a friend's place."
    "Which friend?"

"A friend."

I knew that one thing that irked her—one among several—was when I talked back to her, so, just as I had calculated, I was punished: straight to bed without dinner. It was just as well; the soup and rice had been more than enough.

**PART OF MY** life, and all my daydreams, took place up above, but that didn't mean I could abandon the life I lived down below. So, I went along with my mother to the neighborhood council meeting, as I did every month. There were quite a few kids. We weren't there to listen, we were there for the sandwiches and cookies that were offered around at the end. It was all served with sodas, or coffee for those who felt the cold. The final point was nonnegotiable, as had been made clear the time the neighbor from 3A took along a case of wine, little plastic cups included, and a group of neighbors threatened to throw him out—not just out of the meeting but out of the housing complex—for attempting to "promote alcoholism among the population." We kids exchanged glances, and I think several of us weren't sure whether "population" meant the population of the housing complex or the whole world. We imagined our neighbor handing out his little cups of wine in countries we most likely would never see, but which we knew by heart and recited in history and geography classes: "Austria. Hungary. Czech Republic, Croatia, Italy, Poland, Ukraine," and all the countries of the old Austro-Hungarian Empire, drunk on account of our neighbor.

The meeting always began with the agenda, which the secretary on duty jotted on the board. This time it was:

1. Public lighting
2. The homeless
3. Children's Day
4. Ramón

What they said, following the same order, went roughly as follows:

1. More lights were needed, because the neighborhood was getting more dangerous by the day. Lights on the fences. Lights along the streets. Lights that illuminated everywhere, even beneath the concrete. What for? So nobody would end up handing over their life along with their purse. That was what for. Are we getting a bit carried away, influenced by the news? Neighbor, since you're so rational, you tell me: That group that gathers on the corner at nighttime, what do you suppose they're doing, exchanging poems?

2. The homeless needed to be moved on, before it was too late and the cardboard neighborhood put down roots on the banks of the canal. Had everybody else smelled the campfire smoke? They needed

to live someplace, that was understandable, but did that place have to be right here, when there was so much city to go round? Would there ever come a day when they could get a little peace? The homeless? somebody asked. No, all of us living in the housing complex. Well, the homeless too, and since they were on the topic: peace for the entire world.

3. Balloons and candy needed to be bought for Children's Day, which would be celebrated on the court, or in the clubhouse if it rained. (It had rained last year, when everybody went home soaking wet and, even worse, with a hell of a temper. They had put so much effort into the preparations—balloons, a movie, candy—and everything had gone terribly, as it did whenever they made plans. It had gone so terribly that there were several grown-ups— and when they said "several grown-ups," everyone glanced at the neighbor from 3D, a fiery lady who

was famous for being heavy-handed—who, once they got home, took it out on the objects of celebration. Nobody wanted that to happen again.)

4. Finally, since yet again Paulina hadn't made an appearance, they needed my mother to talk to her, to get her to pass on a message to Ramón. Please could he dismantle that ridiculous eyesore of his. What would people think when they saw it? That everyone around here was a misfit? No, they were respectable people who bathed in the morning, worked during the day, and slept at night. True, there were a few layabouts, as there were anywhere, but for one of those layabouts to be the first thing they saw every morning when they looked out their windows—well, that was something else entirely. What would the children think? And what kind of job was it, anyway, just being there, doing nothing? He can live wherever he pleases, somebody piped

up, and the neighbor from 2B waved his hand in the air, as if trying to brush that comment away.

The meeting ended, as always, with us kids fighting over the sandwiches. I remember that when we reached our building again, my mother pressed Paulina's doorbell, but nobody answered. And I remember she said, talking to herself, not me, "Where could that woman have got to?"

I knew that most likely "that woman" was in the billboard house, so when my mother went over to the window once we were inside the apartment, I asked if she could please help me with my math homework. "Now's not the time for homework. You'll have to sort it out tomorrow," she said, and, with that, she did as I hoped: she forgot what she had gone to the window to peer at and, with a yank, drew the curtain.

**THE THING ABOUT** my mother was that it might be possible to dodge her for a while, but never to escape. So, the following day, Paulina got a barrage of messages telling her to come over because my mother needed to speak to her. When she finally knocked on the door, both had had the whole day—a beautiful day—for their anger to build up.

I can't reproduce the conversation that followed because instead of hanging around to listen, I shut myself in my room. I didn't want to know. But it wasn't much use because, as I've already explained, sound traveled through those walls without asking permission. "Eyesore," "dirty," "lazy" were some of the words my mother spat out, as if she were a sort of parroting machine that worked pro bono for the neighborhood council.

Maybe at that point I should have noticed the way Ramón and the homeless were starting to share the same galaxy, known as "the problem," but I didn't. Instead, I focused on Paulina's retort to my mother, whether angry or sad, I wasn't sure: Ramón was not bothering anyone. He had a right to live however he wanted. The layabouts were them.

The last thing I heard was a door slam. And my mother shouting, "So stupid!"

I didn't know if Paulina heard her. I didn't know if she cared, or if, after thirty years of violent displays of affection and concern, everything reached her in the form of an echo. Coming as it did from so far away, it made a hollow sound.

That same night Paulina's shadow climbed the ladder that connected the earth to the billboard house.

"I'm afraid, Ramón."

"Of what, Pauli?"

"Of something happening to you."

"Like what?"

"I don't know, but they don't like you being up here."

"Who don't?"

"People in the housing complex."

"They won't come up here, don't worry."

"And how do you know?"

"I just do."

Paulina smiled reluctantly, and the two shadows took a seat, this time not holding hands, this time separated by a piece of night.

**ONE OF THE** things I realized around that time was that all human beings are very alike. In other words, if one human takes an interest in something, it's likely that this something will attract others' interest too.

Maybe that explained the looks I kept getting from the other kids the day of the neighborhood council meeting, and the ones they timidly began to cast my way in the schoolyard. It wasn't that these were different from the looks I usually got, because in all truth nobody took much notice of me—it was that they were looks that hadn't been there before.

Sometimes the billboard man was joined by a woman and, most impressively, a boy. They had seen it through their windows, and with their own eyes: the boy didn't use a ladder of any kind, he flew up there. The boy could take a swig from the huge Coca-Cola anytime he wanted. The boy could ride in planes free of charge, because as well as a boy, he was a bird, a pilot, and an astronaut. I think the questions that ensued were a warning. And I should have paid attention. But I didn't.

"Is it you, Miguel?" my classmates asked.

I looked at them as if I didn't follow.

"Is it really you, Miguel?" they persisted.

I didn't say it was. But I didn't deny it either.

**A HALO OF** importance feels especially precious to those of us who have never been important. It called for me to walk a path that until then hadn't interested me in the least: a path of courage and independence. In concrete terms, a boy climbing up the billboard with his aunt following two rungs behind was not the same thing as a boy climbing up alone. And if I did it sure-footed and confident and one of the kids who now looked at me in the schoolyard saw—hopefully one of the younger ones, who were more impressionable— then all the better.

"What are you doing here, Miguel?" asked Ramón when he saw my head appear.

"I just came by to say hello," I answered.

Instead of giving me a sermon on the hazards of heights and then telling me to climb down, Ramón cleared the table and made me a cup of tea, so I pulled out my exercise books and started doing my homework. Due to some oversight—a frequent occurrence among our teachers—after moving through a few chapters in the history and geography textbook, we had backtracked to the Latin American capitals. Brazil: Brasília; El Salvador: San Salvador; Guatemala: Guatemala City; Panama: Panama City. On reaching "Mexico: Mexico City," any moderately sharp student would realize that if the person responsible for naming the capitals hadn't put a whole lot of effort into doing their job, then there was no reason to put any effort into persisting with the homework task.

"And the mud city?" asked Ramón, after hearing me recite the names aloud.

"It's not on the map," I responded, laughing.

Ramón fell silent. And maybe it was this silence, combined with the elevation, that prompted my mind to climb down. I made myself tiny and walked along the crooked, battered streets of the city that the girl and her brothers were still molding at the foot of the billboard. "There's one house too many, we're short a street," said a god of sodden earth who, accustomed to talking to himself, didn't expect his opinion to be heeded by any civilization. "There's one building too many, we're short a door." When I glanced down, I saw that the children from the other day were there once again.

"What time do they come?" I asked.

"At the end of the day," said Ramón.

"And what time is that, roughly?"

"At seven, I guess?"

Departing the earth had its drawbacks because you cast off any extra weight. The clock, for example.

"I went to the neighborhood council meeting," I said.

"And did they elect you president?" asked Ramón.

"They spoke about you and the homeless."

"Want to know what they said?"

"There they are again."

"Who?"

"Those two stars up there."

Ramón explained that they appeared every other day, which he interpreted to mean that there was an interval during which celestial bodies decided between being sedentary or shooting. "A test period," he added.

"Shooting? Shouldn't that be nomadic?" I asked.
  "That's it," said Ramón.

"That's it," he repeated. And we sat down to peer at the thread connecting the sky to the hills. Nomadic people, like shooting stars. A sedentary sky. Brazil: Brasília; El Salvador: San Salvador; Guatemala: Guatemala City; Panama: Panama City; Mexico: Mexico City, I mentally recited. "We're short a door. There are two windows too many," said one of the boys in the distance, imitating the girl.

Several centuries elapsed. I realized it was time to climb down when I felt my stomach rumble.

**BEFORE GOING HOME,** I went by my mother's store with a hankering for cookies. My mother acknowledged me without raising her eyes from her "list of shame," a little sign she carefully stuck to the door the second week of each month. Itemized beside debtors' names were soaps, light bulbs, salt, sugar, tomato sauce (never cigarettes: such a vice), and everything else that had walked out the door "on credit" and hadn't been paid by the agreed date, the first week of the month. This grievance method, designed by my mother, sought to combat shamelessness. "Now everybody can know. And pay," she would say as she worked out the totals in pesos on the calculator.

José Álvarez: $28,235
Sonia Aguilar: $14,720
Andrea Bravo: $3,160

When she got to Beatriz Castillo ($12,300), she said: "Come here, Miguel," and started sniffing my sweater. "You smell like smoke," she said, and fell into a sort of trance that gave me time to add a packet of Doritos to the cookies I had swiped.

"I'm off," I said.

"As soon as you get home, put that sweater in the washing machine."

"It's my school one."

"As soon as you walk through the door, Miguel."

My mother had an aversion to lots of things: the dust that accumulated on the canned-food shelf no matter how many times a day she cleaned it; the stray dogs that, with all the space they had to roam, decided to fall asleep right on the store doorstep. And a whole host of other ills that she grouped beneath the umbrella "delinquency." But there was one last thing, the smell of smoke, and this called for a more refined, sublime category: hate. So, while my sweater went round and round in the washing machine of her mind, she, who had shrunk to the size of a button, moved down passageways that led to scenes still ingrained in her memory, despite her attempts to forget them.

Because the thing is, there was a time when we were the homeless. A time when I wasn't born yet, but my mother was. So she knows exactly what she is talking about, because she was the one (along with Paulina, but Paulina doesn't count because back then she was too little to understand anything) who arrived here, tired, dirty, her feet covered in blisters, walking with the rest.

It just so happened that back in "*that* place" where they lived, there was no work, no food, no nothing, so they had to leave it behind. They had to get as far away as possible, so they wouldn't end up shriveling into nothing in the middle of nowhere. They walked along the long road that led to the city. They walked until their shoes fell apart. Not that it made much difference—their shoes had been broken for as long as they could remember. They walked, walked, walked until they arrived. It took them ten days. Ten days of exhaustion, grief, and thirst.

Whenever the story got an airing, there was always one of those faith-in-humanity types who asked:

"Did anybody give you water?"

## HOW TO TURN INTO A BIRD

"What?"

"Did anybody give you water when they saw you arrive?"

No, nobody gave them water. So, tired as they were, they had to find water, bread, cardboard, and sticks for their fire, which they lit in the same place now occupied by the new group of homeless people. The voice of the neighbor from 4A pulled my mother from her thoughts.

"Are they still there?" she asked, as if it were obvious that since the first shanty went up nobody thought about anything else.

"They are," responded the neighbor from 3B, who came by at the same time every day to buy cigarettes.

"What about the other one?" the neighbor from 4A said, meaning Ramón.

"He's still there too."

"He must be stupid . . ."

"Or intelligent," said the neighbor from 3B, and left, his cigarettes in hand.

**THAT SAME NIGHT,** or maybe it was the following, I heard my mother talking to somebody on the telephone.

"A boy? Up the billboard?"

"It must be one of those grubby new arrivals."

"A boy from the housing complex?"

I remember I switched off the light earlier than usual and put to use a relaxation technique we were taught in gym class. You close your eyes. You inhale. The fences that surround the school disappear. You exhale. You replace the fences and windows with trees. You inhale. The school crest that's painted on one of the walls—a torch illuminating a book—

fades. You exhale. Where the torch was, a crow appears. You inhale. The noise of the buses traveling along the streets at that time of day transforms into the wind in the treetops. You exhale. You turn into an animal from the future. You inhale. A blue cat that knows how everything ends, and for that reason has the gift of serenity.

**LAVENDER, JASMINE, MEADOW** flowers, mango. When I went to meet Paulina at Superior, I found her arranging one of her compositions, this time with the liquid soaps.

"You're going to have to wait awhile, the replenishment stock just arrived," she said.

"Are we going to Ramón's?" I asked.

"I don't know."

"You don't want to?"

Paulina looked at me and seemed like she was about to explain something, but then she passed her hand over her forehead and kept arranging the liquid soaps on the shelves. I knew her well, so her tired gesture didn't fool me. Paulina kept quiet, kept concentrating on the liquid soaps because she didn't trust words, or else because she had noticed that every one of them—the word "love," for example—came with its own set of shelves. It wasn't possible to update the inventory with every phrase. Instead of explaining yourself, you got tangled up.

"Are we going or not?" I persisted.

"Maybe, but let me finish here, Miguel."

Paulina understood the nature of words, she had an eye for color combinations, and she didn't give in to pressure. There was no denying I was at a disadvantage. But I'd never been one to beg, so I went for a wander around the other aisles while she finished, and while she made up her mind whether we would go by Ramón's. It didn't matter.

It wasn't like I needed her permission. And now that I thought about it, I kind of regretted coming here to find her. Annoyed at myself, I was walking down the drinks and dairy products aisle when the guard appeared.

"Hey, kid, you know the saying that goes 'Don't bite the hand that feeds you'?"

"No," I said.

"In that case, repeat after me: I must not bite the hand that feeds me."

"I must not bite the hand that feeds me," I repeated, not understanding.

"That's it, kid. Now add: I must bite the owner of that hand directly on the neck and not let go until I'm sure I've ripped a hole in his jugular." He slipped a Sahne-Nuss into my pocket.

"Thank you," I said to the guard. And I did a ceremonial bow that I immediately regretted, because it was one thing to thank him for sharing his wisdom and quite another to give misleading signs of complicity.

When I went back to Paulina's aisle, the detergent shelf stacker was looking at her handiwork.

"You're an artist, Pauli," he told her.

"Is that a compliment or an insult?" responded Paulina.

"Have you finished?" I interrupted.

"What a pain this son of mine has turned out to be," she said as she set the last bottle in place (lime green), all the while imitating the effect of a slow-motion camera.

**WHEN WE FINALLY** arrived at the billboard, we found Ramón feeding bread crumbs to a small bird that was walking across the table. I'm not sure whether I was more impressed by how at ease the bird seemed so close to him, or by how fast the little hill of beer cans had grown—it was starting to look like the Andes.

"It arrived three days ago," said Ramón in a soft voice, referring to the little bird, as if he were introducing a shy childhood friend. I was trying to decide whether I should respond to him or make like the man who communicates telepathically with animals when Paulina said:

"We just came by to say hello. I'm spent."

"One of the wings is crooked," responded Ramón.

"One of Paulina's?" I said to be funny, but neither of them joined in.

I filled the silence that followed with an unspoken question and conclusion. The question: Was cross-species communication really possible? The conclusion: Paulina was tired, but not only from work at Superior.

Just as she had warned, it wasn't long before she wanted to climb down. And although I knew it wasn't wise to add more tension to the elastic band that was starting to tauten between Paulina and herself—Ramón and his new friend didn't seem to notice anything—I said that I wanted to stay a bit longer. Instead of telling me to climb down, she said: "If that's what you want." And she left.

I sat down next to Ramón to look at the stars.

"Do you think anybody lives up there?" I asked.
"The night is a really big place," he responded.
"And in that case?" I persisted.
"In that case, they could."
"And what would they live in?"
"Coca-Cola billboards?"
"Could they really have reached such heights?" I said as a joke.
"Human beings?"
"No, Coca-Cola."

After a while I said goodbye and walked along the edge of the canal, imagining what would happen if instead of heading back to the housing complex

I kept going straight and didn't stop for hours, days, and years. It was always possible that the road didn't go in a straight line but in a circle that would bring me right back to where I started. Just the thought made me panicky.

Before going home, I went to see Paulina for a bit. She was still acting strange.

"Don't worry, Ramón will come down soon," I remember I said.

"He won't come down."

"Ever?"

"I don't think so."

I was quiet as I went home, quiet as I ate my dinner, and I stayed that way until it was time for bed.

## HOW TO TURN INTO A BIRD

I fell asleep and dreamed that Ramón showed up, speaking in a language nobody understood. One of the neighbors came out of his apartment dressed in red and said that he was sure the language was "Northern German." "You're wrong: it's a dialect from Montevideo," responded the cigarettes neighbor, who was observing the scene from a treetop. Ramón pointed at the sky, and the birds started flying in circles, as if they held the piece that was missing from the conversation.

**I DON'T KNOW** if it was the next day or the day after that, because whenever I cast my mind back, I tend to compress or stretch out the billboard period. Cut, match, and mend—that's what my memory does whenever it happens upon a hole somebody could fall down. Paulina. Ramón. Me.

Children's Day was almost upon us, so I spent the afternoon carrying bags of potato chips and corn puffs. My mother knew where to buy them at a reduced price, so every year she was in charge. And every year, the same thing happened: Everybody said, Let's have balloons, let's have cakes, let's have a Santa Claus suit, but then it was left up to her to chase the neighbors for payment. It was left up to her to do the subtractions and additions and carry the bags. Her, her, her. I was just the ear copping the complaints and the arm dragging some of the bags.

When I was done, worn out as I was, I said I had to go retrieve an exercise book I'd loaned one of my classmates.

"Which classmate?" she asked.

"Donoso," I lied confidently, and before she could say anything further, I set out in the direction of the billboard.

I found Ramón seated, looking toward the highway. Not wanting to disturb him, I made my own tea.

"Like my garden, Miguel?" he asked after a while.

"What garden?"

"This one," said Ramón, indicating the horizon above the hills.

"It's not a garden."

"What do you mean? I planted all the light bulbs. Look how quickly they came up."

It had grown dark, and Ramón wasn't wrong: lights were shining from windows, posts, and the cars that passed along the highway at that hour, and they looked like bright lemons and oranges that an absentminded gardener had let fall to the ground in the garden-night.

"I'll take half a kilo," I said after a while.

"Half a kilo of what?"

"Of lights."

I wanted to ask him when he was coming down. To tell him about the conversation I'd had with

Paulina on the topic, but no words came out of my mouth. The reason? The silence was good. At that hour it was interrupted only by the noise of the odd car, and this time I had gone looking for it, same as Ramón. I let my weariness dissolve in the landscape and climbed down without disturbing him.

On my way back to the housing complex, I bumped into the girl from the shanties. This time she had a ball and was playing alone.

"Your mother didn't come?" she asked.

"No," I said, even though I knew she was referring to Paulina. "And your brothers?" I attempted to join in with the construction of imaginary families.

"I don't know," said the girl. "Why does your father live up there?" she continued, making it clear that she was the one who asked the questions.

"Because he looks after the lights," I said, passing over this new misunderstanding.

"All of them?"

"All of them," I confirmed, and told her the story of his garden.

It was while I was walking toward the housing complex that I remembered where I'd seen the girl. Paulina had a photo of an excursion to the beach. Her whole grade had been put on a bus and taken to see the ocean. Sixty or seventy children who shouted the whole way there. When they jumped out of the bus, the teacher told them to run, and they obeyed: they ran until they came upon an immense stretch of water that left them speechless and paralyzed. They were like that for a few seconds. And then they resumed their shouting, they waded in (beneath their clothing they were wearing blue bathing suits that the school had bought them), they made castles with the damp sand, and they ate their chicken-and-egg sandwiches.

Before the excursion was over, the same teacher told them to gather together and look at the camera. A souvenir, she said, when a week later she moved among their desks handing out a copy each. Paulina still had hers.

In the photo she was nine or ten years old. A similar age to the mud-city girl, who had the same squinty eyes and skinny legs. They were very alike, so alike that they were really the same girl.

I didn't have a teacher like Paulina's, but I did have neighbors.

The morning of the Children's Day celebration, we woke to a cloudless sky, so, as was agreed at the meeting, some of the neighbors carried the large table to the court and the contents of the bags were placed atop it: potato chips, cookies, and cake. When everything was ready, we finally heard the call we had been waiting for. I don't know if it was louder than in previous years, or if we shouted too much as we ran in the direction of the court. But the fact is, the invitation rang out across the streets of the housing complex, across the highway, and reached the banks of the canal.

I remember some of the smallest kids were playing beneath the table, a group had stood up to go play, and I was making up my mind whether to join them or keep eating when the girl and her brothers appeared.

"Can they join?" she asked, indicating the two boys. Her expression was serious, as if instead of a girl she were an old lady who, wearied by life, wasn't in the mood for games.

There was silence. The twins from 2C and I shuffled along to make space for them, but another voice, meant for us, said: "Stay put." Another silence, and then another voice, coming from my mother or one of the neighbors, added: "This celebration is only for children from this housing complex."

"You're not missing anything here. So: off you go."

"But . . ." said the neighbor from 3B. She didn't manage to finish her sentence because someone, I don't know who, hushed her.

The girl looked first at the adults and then at us. She took her brothers by the hands, spat on the ground, and said, "We're leaving." The children from the shanties slowly walked away, and when they got to the sidewalk, one of them threw a stone and made a noise that sounded like a laugh. The stone landed near the table but didn't touch us. It didn't break the heavy silence that had settled between the cups and plates either.

We tried to get on with the festivities, but the food got stuck in our throats, so, after a while, most of us made up an excuse to go home: "I need to go to the bathroom"; "I'm just going to go find a sweater"; "My tummy's sore."

The sun went down.

The sun came up.

And the table, which the next day was still abandoned on the court, had taken on the look of a dying animal that should have stayed in the forest but, out of poor judgment, had ended up taking its final breaths on that rectangle of cement.

I went to see if I could find the girl and her brothers. I did a few laps but didn't venture too far. Now that my neighbors had thrown them out, the logical thing would be for their neighbors to do the same to me. Some things in life follow a predictable pattern.

Because my search had brought me near the billboard, I took the opportunity to climb up and tell Ramón what had happened, but the bird was hopping around again, and he seemed more interested in observing it than in listening to my story. A while later he said:

"Sometimes a family of cats comes by. A big one and three small ones. Looking for food scraps,

I think. A few days ago, a skinny, mottled one appeared, and it tried to join the group. Know what they did?"

"No."

"Meowed and scratched it."

"Why?"

"Don't know. There are plenty of mice running along the banks of the canal to go around."

"Then why did they act like that?"

"At first I thought it could be sick, and the group was protecting itself."

"Was that it?"

"No, because the cat still slinks around on its own."

"What was it, then?"

Ramón didn't respond. Seated, not looking anywhere in particular, I felt as weary as a hundred-year-old man who, sick of moving his skin and bones, perishes in the seclusion of his bedroom. Sometime later, when somebody remembers he exists and goes over to see him, the only thing they find is a mound of dust. So, that somebody takes a broom and sweeps, trying to make the space as spick-and-span as possible. Then they write a sign that they hang in the window, which reads: FOR LEASE.

From up above, life showed you its transparent threads. Sometimes you wanted to open your eyes and follow their course. At others, you preferred to squeeze your eyes shut and not let in any kind of light.

"Don't you get sad, being up here by yourself?" I asked, moved by a sense of sorrow I couldn't shake.
   "No."

Ramón's monosyllables and silences forced me to find the answers to my questions. This time, the answer went roughly like this: it didn't matter if you were a young boy or a decrepit old man, down below you didn't have any more company than what you had up here.

From the other side of the building windows, several people watched and imagined our conversation. Most of them murmured a chorus: "Mad." But there were others—more of them every day— who thought Ramón's idea wasn't so terrible after all. Those were the dangerous ones. And this would be addressed at the next neighborhood council meeting, together with stone throwing, both included under the agenda item "Child safety."

**WHEN WE GOT** to the meeting, the agenda, already noted on the whiteboard by the secretary on shift—one of those people who write oh so neatly while dreaming about the planet finally blowing apart—was the following:

1. The homeless
2. Child safety
3. Public lighting
4. Ramón

1. The homeless had to go. They couldn't wait for the municipality to come up with a solution because how long would that take? Five years? Ten? How long had it been before the residents

of the housing complex escaped that same wind-swept patch of dirt? They had tolerated seeing the homeless from their windows because, when it came down to it, the homeless weren't to blame for the "situation" they were in. And anyway, the curtains could always be drawn when it came time for them to light their fires. But violence, now that was not something the residents would stand for. This time it had only been children, but what would happen if next time the ones wielding the stones were adults? No, the homeless weren't to blame, but who was? God? The mayor?

2. They weren't doing it for themselves but for the children. And everyone knows bad habits are contagious, like measles or head lice. They couldn't just stand by as those people contaminated what they most loved and cared for. Hadn't they heard about the single rotten apple spoiling the whole

bushel? The children were the apples of the housing complex and the hope of the world. Moreover,
there was the matter of the canal. What would
happen if, foolish as the children were, they got
the idea to go play with the little brats, and ended
up at the bottom of the canal? It hadn't happened
of late, but that didn't mean it could never happen again. Had they forgotten Eduardito, the boy
who drowned? There was one other child-related
issue that they would address when they reached
agenda item number four.

3. They needed the lighting urgently. The request
had been put to the municipality more than a
month ago, and they had been promised an inspec-
tion. When? That same week. No, nobody showed.
The number they were assigned was B345. Could
someone volunteer to chase that down? And then
we kids, committed to honing our collective-

thinking skills, imagined the neighbor from 1A trying to lasso a cluster of letters and numbers that were fleeing up the stairs. "They won't get away now that I'm on their tail!" shouted our neighbor.

4. Ramón. When did Ramón intend to come down from there? The matter was simple: if a given individual wanted to live in the housing complex or its surroundings, they had to do so like a person, not like an animal. Had they seen his beard? Did anybody really believe he was paid to sit up there, doing nothing? There were two more things. The first: a journalist had asked at the store if anybody knew the billboard man. They said none of them did, but what would happen if he kept investigating and found out Ramón was one of them? Would it be on the news? The last thing they needed was for that birdhouse to become a tourist attraction. Though that wasn't such a bad

idea, said the wine-in-little-cups neighbor. They responded in unison, with a question: Did good, honest people sleep in houses or hang from the trees? And without waiting for a response, they moved on to the final topic: they had seen a boy up the billboard. "A boy?" asked the neighbor from 2B. "Yes, a boy," responded the wine-in-little-cups neighbor, who, despite the hostile atmosphere, insisted on participating.

**WHEN WE GOT** back to the apartment, I shut myself in my room to devise a plan to disappear. There was still time for me to curb my growth, pass for a gnome, and get lost among the bushes forever. I was considering this when my mother opened the door and looked at me with an expression of: I know the boy is you, because no matter how you try to hide it, I know everything you have done, are doing, and will do, even with my eyes closed. Never forget, Miguel, that I was the one who gave birth to you. Not your father. Not Paulina. I did that.

I lowered my gaze quickly because I knew my mother could see into the past, in large part because of her habit of living in it. But could she do the same with the future? If that was the case, had she always known what would happen? And did "always" mean from the day she was born? I know the boy is you, I heard for the second time in my head, thanks to the unpleasant journey her thoughts could make from her brain to mine.

I thought she would pull my hair or make me go to bed without dinner, but she only said that tomorrow, after school, she needed my help at the store.

"What about my homework?" I asked.

"You can do it there," she said. Then she added: "Where I can keep an eye on you."

**I FORBADE MYSELF** from visiting Ramón. I had come to realize that anybody could become the rejected cat, depending on the group's mood. And although I was pretty sure that deep down this didn't increase or diminish the solitude the cat carried around on its back, something told me it was better to be cautious.

I tried to focus on school: we had skipped ahead in the textbook again until we came to the Industrial Revolution. "Viva!" the teacher said. "Viva!" we kids shouted, standing on our chairs, in a sort of spontaneous homage to our teacher's enthusiasm and to people's struggles. We were accustomed to viewing adults as beings who never reacted, so these struggles really fired our imagination. It was a shame the textbook only ever talked about events that happened so long ago and someplace else. In any case, we showed our solidarity.

Once more I concentrated on dodging the plates, real and imagined, that my mother threw at the walls. Paulina's sadness, too.

"What's wrong, Pauli?"

"What do you mean?" she responded as we walked from the supermarket to the store, a few perfumes in hand. The transaction wasn't the least benefit to her because my mother never paid her back. It didn't matter. Paulina preferred to make that sacrifice for the sake of not having to listen to my mother's complaints about the customers, the manufacturers of those same perfumes, and a long etcetera that ended up including all of humanity.

"Are you sad?"

"A bit."

I understood, without Paulina needing to say anything, that it was about Ramón.

They had been neighbors forever but hadn't taken much notice of each other until the day he stepped inside her classroom, no books in hand, his hair uncombed. It was as if he were the last of an unidentified species that had just landed, confused, dressed in the school uniform, unsure what he was doing there or what was expected of him. From that moment on, they had never been apart.

People who fall in love know that every relationship implies effort. Who had made the greater one? Faced with that question, Ramón, who never said anything, would take the floor and respond:

"Paulina." She, who was normally the one who talked, would keep quiet. She had anchored Ramón to the earth from that very first day, and he, who loved her back, had let himself be anchored.

"I'm tired."

Yes, I'd known her since I could remember, and it was true that she was tired: of carrying the perfumes, of arranging products on the shelves, and of keeping hold of the thread that kept Ramón tethered to the earth. There was something else: for a while now, she had been telling the story of the two of them—to others, but above all to herself—in the past. And most of the time, as she had learned from the same teacher who took her to see the ocean, the past was a complex verb tense.

## HOW TO TURN INTO A BIRD

Bird: A creature with feathers and wings,
usually able to fly.
Man: A rational living being, male or
female. Prehistoric man.

They were not the same thing. A man and a bird
were not the same thing. I had discovered this by
searching the dictionary, but the last thing Paulina
needed was one of those always ill-intentioned
I-told-you-sos. Because everybody had told her,
and she, stubborn as she was, hadn't listened. Were
they right? It didn't matter. They could all go singing in a line to the top of the same hill that Ramón
enjoyed gazing at so much.

This indifference to others' opinions was what
Ramón liked most about her. That, and her ability to find a different combination for the health
and beauty aisle products every day. He was con-

vinced that it was the order inherent in the colors of the bottles she handled—not the rotation and movement of the planets—that allowed the world, strange and absurd as it was, to keep turning. From the height the billboard gave him—ten meters—everything proved simple and clear. So, he wouldn't come down.

Paulina understood. Maybe the dictionary was wrong not to include intermediate species. Because there were bird-men, fish-women, and wolf-boys who spent their lives searching for hideaways where they could stretch their wings, swim around, lick their fur. But she wasn't in charge of the dictionary. Nor was he, or anybody they knew.

There had been no recriminations. Only a pent-up sobbing, which they had let out while holding hands so that it would hurt less. It had hurt just as much.

## HOW TO TURN INTO A BIRD

"Please take care of yourself," Paulina had said as she dried the last of her tears on her sweater sleeve. And Ramón had looked at her without saying anything. In a language that had needed fewer words with the passing of each day, that look had meant: You too.

When we finally arrived at my mother's store, we asked her for the key to where the perfumes were kept. Brut, Natalie, Gelatti. I took care of taking them out of the bag, and Paulina took care of arranging them. Coral, 351, Magic. By the time we got to Jean les Pins, I couldn't say that our arrangement of the perfumes had helped sustain life on earth, but I could say that I had just lived through the saddest afternoon in the world.

"Can I give you the money for those at the end of the month?" said my mother.

"All right," said Paulina.

**RAMÓN'S THEORIES WERE** always a bit confusing, maybe because not even he was all that interested in them. But there were rules to live by too, and these stood out for their precision and clarity. One of them: sometimes the only way to alleviate profound sorrow is to get sloshed. So, for three days and three nights he drank as much beer as he could and said goodbye to Paulina.

In the absence of other people, the conversation that Ramón had with himself moved through stages of flow, even happiness, that would have been impossible without the generous company of alcohol. Through dark places too—stammering, tears, hiccups—that were useful in their own way.

For what? Only he knew. After all, he alone trod the path of his drunkenness. A rocky path—all the world's drinkers know as much—but as illuminating as any of those traveled by the great sages of the Jesus Christ or André the Giant variety.

**TIME UP ABOVE** started to elapse hazily, above all for Ramón. Time down below, heavy as it was, didn't stop. I'm not sure if everything that happened in the next few days followed the order I remember, or whether I am the right person to tell the story. But suppose it went roughly like this:

The first day—according to the calendar of Ramón's bender—the children from the shanties came to the housing complex, this time chaperoned by an older man, their grandfather maybe, who accompanied them to the court using a stick as a cane and carrying a bag.

The man settled himself on a wooden bench with all the majesty of kings we had never seen but had certainly imagined. Once he was comfortable, he said loudly and gruffly: "You can play here." The children, who had brought a ball, did what they were told, and for a good while they were occupied with what looked like a soccer match against an opposing team that only they could see. The neighbors, from their windows, watched the game without daring to repeat the words they had said on Children's Day. I think that this—swallowing their words—rankled them even more than the unexpected visit. On top of that, the old man inspired in them a feeling that had been forgotten for so long it was unrecognizable, and, for that reason, annoyed them: respect. The bearded, ragged old man inspired their respect. They couldn't fathom it, and to be honest, they weren't all that interested in trying to.

"Is it Santa Claus?" asked the boy from 4D from his window.

"Moron," responded the neighbor from 2A.

"My son is no moron," said the boy's mother at the same time as she gave him a push so she could get a better view of what was happening on the court.

"But is it or isn't it?" The boy returned to the subject, from below the table now, more interested in the possibility of obtaining a Christmas present than in anybody else's opinion.

"It's not Santa Claus, it's Bag Man," the girl from 4A corrected him.

When they heard that name, Bag Man, the people looking through the windows fell down a hole in their memories. The old man the children were disparaging was one of their own. One who, when finally they had all been given the long-hoped-for apartments, decided he didn't want his, and that he would stay living where he was, out in the open.

The story had been passed down over a couple of generations: the canal had "captured" the old man. Just as the street or the hill had "captured" others. So, "be very careful." Back then and now, we kids listened, widening our eyes and gulping: everything had a spirit that, instead of protecting us, was there to "capture" us. The sooner we learned it, the better: the community's gods followed the logic of the police.

There was a second explanation that was, if anything, an extension of the first. The old man was guardian of the homeless, a divinity made of mud who carried the filth of the world on his shoulders. They called him "Grandfather," and even if centuries went by, even if the homeless were succeeded by others, he liked to be known by that name always. In his bag was a bottle of aguardiente, which he passed around to the adults on cold nights. Blankets, too, which he settled over the children. These were made from scraps he found in the dumpsters that, when the territories were divided up, had remained in his domain. He called those dumpsters "mis huachitos"—his traps.

The problem was the cold nights when the aguardiente and blankets weren't enough. Nights like that, the old man would have one of his episodes: like a rabid animal, he would rage and bellow, and he would take his stick and hit himself and anybody else who crossed his path. He would have liked to belong to a master who might take pity on him and deliver him a bullet to bring it all to an end. But he was a god, and gods, as well as being immortal, have no masters.

"It's Bag Man," repeated the girl from 4A, and we spectators turned our attention back to the imaginary match. We all understood who had won.

"All right, let's go," said the old man, getting up with the help of the stick. And with that "let's go," he meant: since they haven't said anything this time, I hope they won't do it again when the children come here on their own.

The four of them—the god, the princess, the two princes—left. They walked back toward the banks of the canal. The same day, my neighbors started looking for their own sticks. I'm not sure whether this was in homage to the old man, or whether it was so they could defend themselves from him if he ever returned.

**DONOSO WAS BEHIND** what went down at school. He was the same classmate I used for my lies. My unconscious summoned him, and there he appeared, interrogating me at recess.

A food cart often parked on the other side of the fence. I was stretching my arm through the bars, trying to buy some potato chips, when Donoso grabbed me by the throat and carried me off to the darkest corner of the schoolyard, a.k.a. the police station, where we went for interrogations and beatings. Like we didn't get enough of those at home.

"Are you the one who goes up the billboard?"

"Mind your own business, moron."

That's what I should have said, but instead, trying to act important, I talked about the lights and about how I didn't need my mother's or anybody else's permission to go up there because, for a while now, I was the boss of me. Did that make me the moron? I think, instead, I was an ordinary person who didn't get many chances to appear interesting.

"I'm climbing up too," said Donoso. And by the time he finished, the three mini Donosos who followed him around everywhere had appeared.

"Me too."

"Me too."

"Me too," they echoed.

"What do you want to climb up there for?" I asked.

"To take a piss," responded Donoso, and he gave me a shove on the shoulder that was followed by three snorts of laughter and three mini shoves.

**I WENT LOOKING** for Paulina at Superior and found her in the cereals and canned goods aisle, talking to the guard.

"Hi, kid," he said when he saw me.

"'Miguel' is just as easy to say," I responded.

"Don't be a pain, kid," said Paulina, playing the clown.

A part of me was happy to see Paulina looking a little brighter, but another part, maybe the part more committed to the role of "son," sensed that the guard was a threat. I had seen him walk Paulina to the housing complex with the excuse that he "felt like stretching his legs," as if being on his feet all day didn't do that. I reacted like a furious judge who, not content to ask the questions, starts providing the answers too: A couple of days? Was that all sorrow lasted? The world was a little puff of popcorn, a tiny speck of lint.

I didn't wait for her, and even though I had forbidden them, my feet conveyed me toward the billboard. All my decisions—in this case, my resolve not to climb up there again—had an exceptionally limited expiration date. In that regard I was just like Paulina and everybody else.

When I reached the top, Ramón had his head resting on the table and said to me, "Miguelito." I wanted to help him over to where the hose was connected to the water drum, so he could wet his face, but when I tried to get him to his feet, he fell onto me like a dead, smelly bear. I dragged him to the mattress, removed his shoes, and covered him with the blanket. Disoriented, I switched on the tangle of cables and heated water to make some soup, which neither of us ended up tasting.

"Thank you, Miguelito," he said. And he fell into a deep sleep.

I remember I cried for a while, and my tears made the lights that started coming on seem even brighter than usual. When I blew my nose, I caught my father's scent—a whiff of denim—and it was as if he were sitting beside me, resting a hand on my shoulder. I remembered how a couple of times he got home from work early, and instead of going to the store, we went to the court to kick the ball around.

I didn't want his pity. Much less the pity of his ghost, so I wiped my eyes and decided nothing more could be done up here. I climbed down, and I came across the girl from the shanties. On seeing me so serious, she assumed something out of the ordinary was going on and asked me if my father was sick.

"Drunk sick," I answered her angrily and went on my way, thinking that the next time I would clear up with her that I had no father and Ramón was my uncle.

When I reached the building, Paulina was waiting for me on the stairs. I sat down beside her, and together we finished shedding the tears that had started falling bit by bit.

"Are you sure he's not coming down, Pauli?"
    "Even if he wanted to, he couldn't anymore."
    "Because of the neighbors?"

"Because of himself, Miguel."

One side of love, an undervalued one, has to do with letting the other person walk their own path. Paulina understood this, Ramón understood this, and now it was my turn. So, I dried my eyes, gave Paulina a hug, and went inside.

"That damn smell of smoke again," said my mother.

The same person who, just a few days before, had initiated a pacifist discussion at the most recent neighborhood council meeting shook me and slapped me across the face a few times, until I fell to the floor. I picked myself up and went to my room. I had learned from Paulina that brushing off the words and actions of others was sometimes a matter of life or death.

**IN THE BOOK** of my family, which I'm grateful nobody has gone to the trouble of writing, the smell of smoke gets a special chapter that also features my grandmother, whom I barely remember. Soon after arriving in the city, she found work in a bakery. It wasn't just any job; it was the first job of her new life. Kneading and cutting. Cutting and kneading. She had been doing that for a week or two when a workmate asked her, laughing, if she slept in the middle of a bonfire. He said it would be a good idea to air out her clothes. Or to wash them more often. Because she had running water, didn't she? Or at least windows. Her clothes, she was told, smelled musty.

My grandmother answered yes, of course she had running water, but her face went so red that the bakery owner, who had been listening, realized his new worker was lying. And she, my grandmother, who more than anything else in the world took care of her clothes, who scrubbed them in the washtub until they were white as sacks of flour (just like the ones that were eavesdropping on this conversation and were now laughing at her), had thought her scrubbing did the trick. But no. It was impossible to get rid of the smell because the damned smoke permeated everything. It left you enveloped in a cloud that you could never be rid of. A cloud that was there to tell you where you came from and, most importantly, how far you could go.

"You have running water, don't you?" asked her boss.

"Yes, of course, don't worry," she responded.

## HOW TO TURN INTO A BIRD

He, who found her assurances hard to believe, and who knew she lived by the canal, said she could use the bakery lavatory to wash her and her girls' clothes. The offer only made matters worse.

That evening, my mother and Paulina went to light the brazier, as they always did. But instead of charcoal, matches, and wax, they were given a slap that left them crying, snot all over their faces.

Never. Never again would a fire be lit by the members of that family. The paraffin stove, which my grandmother bought with her first month's wages, would have to be enough. And if it was not, then Paulina and my mother could wrap themselves in blankets. Or they could go to hell.

# THE FINAL DAYS

**RAMÓN HAD GONE** to live up a billboard. Soon after, Paulina had realized he wouldn't be coming down, and instead of asking him to, she had let him go on living up there. I couldn't be mad at them for that. Nobody had told me to believe the joke ("Your son's getting so big!"; "How is your father?"). Nobody had told me to construct an imaginary family that would last an even shorter amount of time than a real one. It wasn't so bad. Anybody who had survived beyond ten years of age as I had was in possession of a carapace as hard as a cockroach's—"My opponent is the world," the Chinese man from the martial arts movie had said. So, a couple of days later, there I was again, up the billboard.

A new wisdom inside me knew it was better not to mention the benders, so I greeted Ramón as usual. I realized his hair had grown, and, bit by bit, he was starting to resemble a Neanderthal.

"Nice beard," I said.

"I was thinking about cutting it," he answered.

"Really?"

I offered to be his barber, and we began with the impromptu trim. Tufts started falling as if they were newborn animals, ready to land on the ground and start exploring. Once we finished with his beard, we followed up with a haircut, and then, inspired as I was, I fixed up my own hair too, snipping the lengths that covered my forehead.

Ramón pulled on his blue shoes and adjusted his coat and said: "Ready."

## HOW TO TURN INTO A BIRD

"For what?" I asked.

"Lolo's bar, so we can have some empanadas."

"You're climbing down?"

"Doubt they'll bring them up here."

**I COULD HAVE** jumped at the chance to ask if there was even a tiny possibility that he might stay down below and move back in with Paulina. But when I looked at him, I understood what Paulina had tried to explain to me a few days before: even if he did climb down, Ramón would continue living in a far-off place. Maybe he had finally seen the threads that connected everything. Or maybe it was just the opposite, and he had established that those threads didn't exist: there were only strands—who knows if these were what remained of an original tapestry—and they, unbound to anything, were spinning loose. Whatever the case, it was a discovery that belonged to him alone.

When we got to Lolo's, the people sitting at the tables were happy to see us. It was as if we had made a long journey and now everybody wanted to know what the country we visited was like, and if we just so happened to have brought back a keepsake.

"Half a dozen cheese empanadas, a beer, and . . ." Ramón looked at me.

"A Bilz soda," I added.

"How have you been, Ramón?" asked Lolo.

"Pretty good."

"So it seems, by the looks of you."

Lolo decided that everything would revolve around the new arrivals for the rest of the afternoon. It was impossible to stay out of the conversation because he and the waiter shouted their questions from behind the bar.

What was life in the billboard like?

Was it cold up there?

Did he need another light source, or were the billboard lamps enough?

Was he the one who switched them on?

What did he do in the daytime?

Since I knew Ramón had decided to embark upon another silent period in his life, I took charge of expanding upon his replies. I remember I described the time of day when the lights started coming on—up there above us, I said, was a brightly lit garden. The cold could be withstood with the help of some soup and, in extreme cases, a blanket. Alcohol helped too. Any light the billboard didn't give off, the stars made up for. I wasn't sure if they'd noticed, but there were two stars in particular that appeared in the sky only every second day. Turned out that the stars, just like some human beings (and here I paused so they would realize that when I said "some," I was referring to the two of us), could choose the kind of life they wanted to live. The light bulbs? They were switched on by a man called Eliseo, who lived in a distant place, and I'm not sure why but instead of naming a Latin American capital I said: Pakistan.

"You've got a great boy there, Ramón," said Lolo.

"He's my nephew," Ramón clarified.

"I don't have a father," I said, proud, and lifted my glass, proposing a toast. "To Ramón. And to the Industrial Revolution," I added, finally finding a use for my history and geography lessons: to bring conversations to a sudden, surprising end. I kept talking with Ramón for a while, and that was what we were doing when the neighbor who bought his cigarettes at my mother's store pulled up a chair, asking if he could join us.

"Take mine. At this time of day, I like to watch the sun set," I said, once again leaving a silence after my words that I hoped would impress my audience.

I remember I said goodbye to Ramón with a simple "chao." There, surrounded by good friends whose names he didn't need to know, he looked content. It was the last time I saw him.

**THE BALANCE STRUCK** between life up above and life down below depended on a system of pulleys and ropes. Even though the whole operation was precarious, it never stopped moving, and it brought about new situations, visible and invisible.

What followed went roughly like this:

From his window, Donoso observed the moment Ramón and I climbed down the billboard, and he decided now was the perfect time to pay the visit he'd been planning for days.

"Who's coming?"
    "Me."
    "Me."
    "Me."

"Me."
"Me."
"Me."
"Me."

Seven boys formed a line behind Donoso, proceeded down the street, and crossed the highway until they reached the banks of the canal.

They didn't know it, but the boy who crossed with them—his clothes, they thought, looked a bit muddy—was the ghost of Eduardito, the boy who had drowned. He wanted to warn them that there are junctions where the line joining the past to the present bends right around until it forms a hole. "If you fall down, you won't come back," he wanted to tell them. But, with all the adrenaline pumping through them, they didn't stop to listen.

## HOW TO TURN INTO A BIRD

I can imagine them climbing the ladder, exploring the billboard house, and then peeping through the hole that served as a window. The rain of urine they launched from the air, too, because just as Donoso had said, their main aim wasn't to gaze at the hills and city from up high, it was to take a piss.

As for what happened next, not even they knew for a fact. Maybe they saw me coming and thought Ramón wouldn't be far behind. Or maybe it was even simpler: once their mission was accomplished, they got scared and hurried down.

Eight boys went out, but only seven came back.

When the Eduardito episode happened I was five, so I don't remember many details. The first: the name, Eduardito, which the grown-ups shouted for three days and two nights straight. The second:

his bloated face, asleep and a bit purple. The third: the satin-lined coffin, which made me think that, if by miracle or mistake Eduardito awoke deep in the ground, his new bed would seem nice and soft. Would he scratch and kick until he broke through it? That nightmare was to chase all us kids who peered at him to say a final goodbye, more out of curiosity than pain, confirming with our own eyes that the dead boy could have been any one of us.

Five minutes, his mother had neglected him for. Five minutes, during which she stepped out to use the neighbor's phone because she needed a tank of propane delivered, and Eduardito, though nobody understood quite how, managed to climb down the stairs, cross the street, and set out for the canal.

Maybe he wanted to put his hands on the shiniest stone he'd ever seen. Or talk to the other Eduardito looking at him from the depths of the water. Nobody knows. Three days, the canal took to return his body. It left it resting, this time forever, between some bushes growing close to the water.

The police came to deliver the news. In a nearby municipality that was intersected by the same canal, the body of a boy had been found. Red-checked shirt. Blue shorts. I thought the scream let out by Eduardito's mother had shattered the windows, but afterward I understood that somebody, maybe his father or elder brother, had dropped the glass he was holding when he heard the news.

"The body of our little angel was so light, too light," repeated his grandmother, trying to explain to everybody who arrived at the wake how the water could have dragged Eduardito so far away. I remember the word "dragged." And I remember that when I accompanied my mother to lay a wreath of flowers, in confusion I stepped into the kitchen in Eduardito's apartment and saw a plate of potatoes that somebody had left half-eaten forever.

**WE KIDS WERE** the first suspects in the disappearance of Jaimito (that was the name of the latest boy to disappear). Nobody was to go to school. Nobody was to move from the housing complex. Nobody was to watch television. Nobody younger than twelve years of age (did we understand?) was to do anything at all until we told them everything we knew.

Did we know him?

Had we seen him that afternoon?

Had we seen anything strange around the housing complex?

Had the cat got our tongues?

Those of us under interrogation, not knowing how to respond, imagined that in fact it was Jaimito's tongue that the cats, blackbirds, and worms were eating.

The problem was, the housing complex was "not what it used to be," as somebody said. Were the homeless to blame? Had they, with their cardboard and sticks, awoken the ghosts that had been put to rest with such trouble in the back room of memory?

(In brief, the ghost of exhaustion,
the ghost of clothing that smelled of smoke,
the ghost of pain.)

Was Ramón to blame? Had he, with his billboard shack, put everything they had been at such pains to order into disarray?

**A NIGHT WENT** by, an entire day, and the boy still hadn't appeared. It must have been the morning of the second day when a neighbor from one building over provided the piece of information that had been missing: children. The day before the disappearance was discovered, while he was looking out the window, he had seen some children playing up there, in the billboard. He was sorry, the neighbor went on, but he no longer thought that Jaimito? Dieguito? what was his name? would be found.

One group set out in the direction of the billboard and another stayed behind to continue the interrogation. The circle of suspects started shrinking until the only ones left inside it were Donoso, two mini Donosos, and me.

What were we doing up there?

Had Ramón invited us?

Did Paulina—the two-faced cow—know anything about this?

They wouldn't let us out of there until we told them everything.

We shouldn't forget that time was slipping away and it depended on us whether Jaimito was found alive or dead. Another question: Whose idea was it to climb up there?

That was when Donoso broke into sobs and said a few words that could barely be made out between one hiccup and the next. They had climbed up. Jaimito had been with them. They knew he had gone with them, but they weren't sure whether he had climbed down. They'd seen somebody who looked like Ramón coming toward them. They had felt scared. They'd climbed down in a flash. They'd thought one of the bigger boys had taken Jaimito's hand, but he mustn't have. "Miguel's, the idea was Miguel's," Donoso finished off.

Would I have gained anything by saying that he was lying, and that I had climbed up, but not with them? No, because what the neighbors had right there, before their eyes, wasn't the people to blame for the boy's disappearance, but the perfect excuse to get rid of Ramón, the homeless, and everything they considered "the problem," once and for all. In other words, to get rid of anything and everything that didn't function according to the laws of the group, which they—as judge and jury—had taken it upon themselves to dictate.

**THE ACTORS IN** the show that was life started running through their lines:

Ramón was to blame. They had said it over and again: Men and women were not birds. Men and women lived in buildings and worked real jobs, and, when night fell, those men and those women watched television, went to sleep in beds, and started snoring. The stars, the night, the wind that blew hardest while they were sleeping—none of that was any of their concern since they had shed their feathers, fur, and carapaces. Because there was a structure, an order to things: Was that so difficult to understand? Was that really so complicated, Ramón?

**I IMAGINE THE** neighbors' thoughts were circling all that, and not the lost boy, when they got down on all fours after interrogating me and started sniffing my clothes.

The head of the pack, who pushed through the door and ran in the direction of our building, was the neighbor from 1A or 4D. I'm not sure. The main thing is, they all went and grabbed the weapons they had hidden beneath their pillows:

> sticks,
> bones,
> fangs.

"You're coming with me," said my mother.

I looked at her, but I didn't say anything.

"Take this stick," she added.

**THEY HAD LEARNED** it in theory and in practice. A good knee to the stomach immobilizes. A broken rib, which hopefully pricks the lung without necessarily puncturing it, is a prompt to be afraid for your life, not just your soul. And, finally, a good kick in the face busts the nose forever. So that you never forget:

What you shouldn't have done.
What you shouldn't have thought.
What you shouldn't have wanted.

(Above all, the final one.)

**ALL OF US**—the group of neighbors, my mother, the father of the disappeared boy, and I—crossed the highway and reached the foot of the billboard. A neighbor who had arrived before we did said Ramón wasn't responding to their shouts for him to come down. The reason was obvious: he was gone.

That didn't mean the show had to stop.

What were they to do now that they had no culprit? How were they to bang a fist on the enormous table that was the world, which, though it didn't belong to them, they took it upon themselves to keep clean and tidy?

The younger adults were tasked with climbing up. We kids weren't forced to help in any way, but we weren't allowed to leave either. This was so the lesson might be etched into the heads full of air—but still free of birds—that we carried around on our shoulders.

I remember that among the crowd were several people who had defended Ramón, now with a stick in hand, saying that he was, that he always had been, a fucking lunatic. Looking at them, I thought this meant that if time kept rolling on, eventually I too would change my mind and feel like killing somebody. With what? With the stone that my hand had just grabbed, a hand that, in my fear and bewilderment, had started acting of its own accord.

**ONE BY ONE,** the objects in the billboard house were brought down in the same order in which a few months earlier Ramón had taken them up: first the mattress, then the two chairs, the small table, and, finally, the lamp. I imagine the mugs and plates were lying abandoned—shivering, maybe—on what had been the floor of the house. Nobody would use them or even see them again, because views from afar had that downside: even if you strained your eyes, you couldn't make out the details.

The sticks the neighbors were holding came in handy when they decided to light a bonfire, where all the belongings, after coming back down to earth—"they should never have left in the first place"—went up in flames. The smoke got in our eyes and then rose skyward, making the billboard's convertible and woman start to blur.

There was a smell of plastic and burnt sky. Did the neighbors calm down once they had destroyed the billboard house?

Of course not.

**THE FIRST THING** I saw when I could open my eyes again was the girl from the shanties. Looking at her, at her hand in Grandfather's hand, I realized I already knew how the uproar that was sure to start in a few minutes would end. How did I know? Because most of the time, the ending is the same.

I think the old man's question was what unleashed the fury: What the hell were we doing?

They responded with a cry: that he should mind his own business, and that he and his filth should go elsewhere.

The next thing, somebody was striking a stick against a head. Two minutes later there were several—on one side and on the other—copying that move. The sticks struck heads. And arms, legs, and backs. Drops of blood fell to the ground, staining it.

Fire. What follows sticks, from the very beginnings of the world, has always been fire, and this fire was still ablaze and was being carried in hand. The cardboard of the shanties burned up quickly.

Cries rang out. From one side and the other. Or sobs, I don't know. At that stage not even the individuals who had started the whole thing and were so sure of being right understood what was happening. Brave as they were, they fled.

## HOW TO TURN INTO A BIRD

The rest of us stayed there, trying to put out the disaster, which lasted between twenty minutes and three thousand years, and which ended with the neighborhood of the homeless reduced, in part, to cinders.

As happens in all wars, after the cries came the silence. I retched, and I dropped the stone that my hand hadn't managed to hurl, and then I dropped the stick my mother had given me, which had served as a cane while my legs shook. Without thinking much about it, I picked it up and passed it to the girl.

This war was not written in any book, but those of us who took part still remember that it started with somebody who was right, and that it was kept alive by words launched to and fro.

**THE NEXT MORNING** the police showed up. They hadn't come about the fire—the firefighters would take care of it, didn't we know that?—but to tell us they had found the body of the lost boy at the bottom of the canal. Once more the only one capable of giving a coherent explanation was the grandmother: "The boy went where he wasn't supposed to go, and then what wasn't supposed to happen happened."

The wake was held in the housing complex. In filed his relatives, the neighbors, and the grandfather of the homeless too. Without saying a word—we insisted on this silent communication system, which we knew was next to useless—we had agreed that in certain circumstances there would be a truce. There was an older lady from a nearby housing complex who always showed up for celebrations and funerals. She looked at the casket, said a few words to God, and slowly shook her head. Jaimito was dressed in a checked shirt, and the button on his collar had been fastened. His mother was seated on a chair and gazed at a horizon only she could see. Somebody, I think it was the neighbor from 3D, started singing a hymn that said heaven and earth would pass away, but not the word of God. Two or three others joined in.

We kids who had taken part in the excursion to the billboard were given a chance to go in to say goodbye, which we did as fast as we could. Though not fast enough to fail to notice that the gladioli, unlike the carnations, looked withered.

## HOW TO TURN INTO A BIRD

I was leaving when I saw Paulina arrive, and I went over to her. She didn't stay long, because my mother took it upon herself to tell her—in the name of nobody, because by that stage Jaimito's family couldn't tell one neighbor from the next— that after what had happened, she wasn't welcome. Me either. So, it would be better if we left. And if it were for good, better yet.

I DON'T KNOW if Paulina made the decision when she heard my mother's words, or whether she made it when, a few days before, the perfume bottles had started clinking against each other, telling her that Ramón's house was on fire.

"Go home and put in your backpack all the clothes that will fit," she said.

"We're leaving?" I asked.

"We're leaving," she replied.

I packed all my briefs, all my socks, two pairs of track pants, and, I'm not sure what for, my school uniform. A pencil and an exercise book, too.

**WE WALKED ALONG** the verge of the highway in the direction of the city center, and bit by bit, we left the housing complex, the clusters of buildings, the factories, and the treeless hills behind.

The lights started blinking on: orange and yellow. Ramón could have been observing those lights from another billboard or from the branch of a tree. There were different theories, but at Lolo's bar at that time of day, the most popular went like this: a few days before, on stepping out the door of that very establishment, Ramón had turned into a bird, a cross between a condor and a crow, and flown away.

There were theories that were even more outlandish: Ramón was working as Eliseo's assistant—Eliseo, the man in charge of the billboards—in the Dominican Republic; Ramón, tired of everything, had thrown himself into the canal; Ramón didn't exist, but had been a collective hallucination produced by the involuntary inhalation of Superior's floor disinfectant. Anything was possible. Or not.

**IN THE FIRST** few days, I imagined my photo, peeling, on one of those flyers that get hung on lampposts. And my mother seated in front of the television, not paying attention to what was happening on the screen, waiting for the day we came through the door so she could punish us in the worst way possible: pretend we didn't exist.

At the hour when the streets in the city center start to empty, Paulina and I steal onto the metro and play at walking along the aisle with our eyes closed. She says: keep going, danger, turn, stop, and I follow her, confident.

Through the speakers a delay is announced, and on the platform opposite, a woman shouts something we don't understand. Paulina has gone quiet, so I open my eyes and look at our reflection in an advertisement for Nike sneakers.

So I won't forget them, I repeat the names of the capitals: Santiago, Lima, Buenos Aires, Managua, Mexico City. It's late, but the air is still warm.

**MARÍA JOSÉ FERRADA**'s children's books have been published all over the world. Her first novel for adults, *How to Order the Universe*, has been translated into nine languages and was named a best book of the year by the *San Francisco Chronicle*, *Southwest Review*, and *World Literature Today*. Ferrada has been awarded numerous prizes and is a three-time winner of the Chilean Ministry of Culture Award. *How to Turn Into a Bird* received the Chilean Art Critics Circle Award. She lives in Santiago, Chile.

**ELIZABETH BRYER** is a translator and writer from Australia. Her translations include Claudia Salazar Jiménez's Las Americas Narrative Prize–winning *Blood of the Dawn*; Aleksandra Lun's *The Palimpsests*, for which she was awarded a PEN/Heim Translation Fund grant; and José Luis de Juan's *Napoleon's Beekeeper*. Her debut novel, *From Here On, Monsters*, was co-winner of the 2020 Norma K. Hemming Award.